The

    peak

        of

            my

                existence

Sofia Rizzo

The

Peak

Of

My

Existence

We'll meet again,

I will love you forever.

You were the peak of my existence

-Caleb brooks

I

Chapter one

---------------------------The audition----------------------------

Hi, I'm Caleb and this day is the most important day of my life. I've never been so nervous. I woke up this morning and the first thing I did was to go wash my face and brush my teeth. My bedroom floor was covered with the homework that I did yesterday since I didn't have enough time to do them today. My window was open and I could feel the cold breeze filling up my room. I went to sit on my bed, that was also covered with a bunch of books. I then put on my favourite pair of jeans and a white shirt. I was late as usual so I ran to the bathroom to do my hair. It looked really messy, but I didn't have time to do it better. I put my contacts in, because I didn't want to audition with glasses on. I heard my sister Maya scream.

"Hurry up Caleb we're late!" so I grabbed my red flannel and ran downstairs.

While still putting on my shoes, I started to go towards the car. My mom was already sitting in there waiting for me and my sister was mad because she had to come back in the house to tell me to hurry. As soon as I closed the car door, my mom drove off.

"Are you nervous, honey?", she asked kindly.

"No, not really", I replied.

She could totally tell I was lying. The thing that made me the most nervous was the fact that I still had to pick a song to sing to the

6

judges. That's when I heard the song on the radio. It seemed like it was made exactly for my voice. "Yellow, by Coldplay".

I knew I had to use this song. I can play the piano and I can sing so I think this is the perfect song for me.

"Mom, I decided the song I'm going to sing, it's the song that just played on the radio."

She looked at me with a weird face. "It's the morning of the audition and you still hadn't decided what song to sing? "

"Well now I know so it's fine", I replied, being a bit disappointed in the fact that she didn't say anything about how good the song is.

We still had to drive for about 40 minutes so I decided to try to sleep a bit. I was so nervous last night that I didn't really get much sleep.

I woke up to my mom calling my name. "Wake up Caleb, we're here". As soon as I opened the car door, I saw a lot of people standing outside of the big red building. There was a shiny sign on top of the building that said: LondonTalents. Almost everyone was accompanied by their family. My mom, my sister and I started to walk towards the long line. We had to wait about 20 minutes until they let us all in. The inside of the building was really big and very illuminated by the daylight. As soon as we walked, in we were approached by a man asking for my name. "I'm Caleb, Caleb Brooks". The man looked for my name on the long list. He was really tall and had a long, black beard. His eyes were dark and big and his hands were going down every name on the list. When he finally saw mine, he looked up and said "This is your number, your audition is at 2:30, if you're late we will move on to the next person and you'll have to come back next year. You can go wait it the waiting room on the second floor. The bathrooms are on the third floor. Your audition will be on the fourth floor." I thanked him and we walked towards the elevator to go to the second floor.

"Maya, I'm going to the bathroom really quick. You and mom can wait for me in the waiting room.".

"Please don't be late Caleb, we are not doing this again next year", she said, sounding a bit worried.

When we reached the second floor, they went out of the elevator and started walking towards the waiting room. The elevator doors closed and I waited patiently until I had reached the third floor. When the doors opened, I walked out into a big hallway. There were a lot of offices. Each door had a name on it, to identify whose office it was. At the end of the hallway, I saw the signs telling me that the bathrooms were on the right. I walked all the way down the hallway, paying attention to the time, since the last thing I wanted to do was to be late. As I turned to the right, I saw a person. I didn't notice them quick enough to stop before bumping into them.

"Oh my god, I am so sorry!" I said, without looking the person in the eyes, since I was way too embarrassed.

"No worries, it was totally my fault. I shouldn't be running but I'm late for my audition."

I noticed that it was a man's voice. He had a very deep voice. I raised my head slowly. The most beautiful man I had ever seen was standing in front of me. He had emerald green eyes. The look he gave me with those eyes made me feel like he was staring directly into my soul. His face was perfectly shaped. His lips had a very light tone of pink. He was wearing a pair of black skinny jeans and a red shirt. He had long, brown and curly hair that he had put into a man bun. "I'm Edward by the way" he said, leaning his hand to me.

I grabbed it a gave him a gentle handshake.

"I'm Caleb, are you auditioning for the show too?" I asked

"Yes, I am... oh my god, I'm late. My audition starts in two minutes. I'm really sorry but I have to go. It was nice meeting you Caleb."

He started to sprint down the hallway and to the elevator, where I saw him nervously waiting for one. When the doors opened, he immediately pressed the 4th floor button and the doors closed.

I was still a bit in shock because of how handsome this man was. I just couldn't get his beautiful eyes out of my mind. In that moment I remembered that I still had an audition to go to. I started running towards the bathrooms. Out of breath, I reached the bathrooms and entered. The inside of this bathrooms was all blue with white waves on the walls. The floor was a bright white and the lights were yellow. This bathroom didn't look new or clean. Since my audition would be starting in 10 minutes, I had to hurry. I walked to one of the bathroom stalls and entered really quick. When I got out of the stall, I looked at the time and almost started to panic. I had just 1 minute to get to my audition. After washing my hands, I got out of the bathroom and started to run. I don't think I've ever been able to run this fast in my whole life. When I got to the elevators, they were not opening. I had 30 seconds left until the beginning of my audition so I decided to take the stairs. I turn to the right and see the door that would lead me to the staircase. I open the door and start running up the stairs. My heartbeat had never been that fast before. When I finally see the door to the fourth floor, I open it and walk into another big hallway. I had to look for the audition room really fast, since my audition had to start now. On my left I saw a door with a sign that said; Audition rooms. I entered the door and suddenly found myself

standing in front of the four judges. I knew I couldn't sing right now; I was completely out of breath

"Can I have 1 minute?" I asked the judges nicely.

The only woman out of the judges slowly nodded and game me a smile.

After a little break and a sip of water, I was ready to sing. I walked to the middle of the room, standing right in front of the four judges. The only woman there had long, blonde hair and bright blue eyes. If I had to guess, I would say she was around 40 years old. The man sitting on her right had white hair and was really old. The man on her left was around 30 years old and had shoulder long black hair. The man that was sitting on the far left was really intimidating. He was staring at me in a really mean way. His eyes were slowly looking at my clothes with a look of judgment. I tried to ignore the looks he gave me and stepped forward to present myself to the judges.

"Hi, I'm Caleb Brooks and I'm from Doncaster." I could hear my voice shaking a bit, so I took a deep breath and tried to calm down.

"Hi Caleb, what are you going to sing for us today?" the woman said, showing me a big smile.

"Yellow by Coldplay."

"Good luck!" I sat down to the piano in the room. As soon as I put my hands on the piano, I took one last deep breath and started to play.

Chapter two

"Wow, that was really impressing!"

The woman with the white sweater got up and started clapping. My audition must have been really emotional to her, since she had tears in her eyes. The man sitting next to her got up too. The man on her right was clapping but didn't bother to get up. The only person that wasn't clapping was the man sitting on the far left. His eyes were still staring at me, in a very judgmental way. I was getting a bit insecure that he didn't like my singing.

"Enough with the clapping now." the man said. "What's your name again?" he asked.

"Caleb"

"Okay look Caleb, your singing wasn't too bad. I don't like how you're dressed and I don't like the song you chose." He said, giving me an evil look.

"Why do you always do this Brad? I'm sorry that he said that to you sweetheart, he doesn't really mean it." The woman suddenly turned towards me. I wasn't sad about what he said, I knew the other judges liked me.

"Let's just go to the voting Sabrina" said Brad, while looking at the woman, with an annoyed face.

"It's a yes for me." Sabrina said

I was so happy to hear those words, but I knew that I wasn't safe yet.

12

"It's a yes for me too." The man next to her gave me a thumbs up.

"It's obviously a no for me." I heard Brad say.

My hearth skipped a beat when he said those words. I knew that if the last judge would give me a no, my dream would be over and I would have to go back home and tell everyone how I failed.

"Look kid, I liked your singing and I think you could really do some good things. It's a yes for me."

When I heard him say that sentence, I fell to my knees. The whole anxiety I had in my body since last night, finally disappeared. I made it, I got into the biggest singing competition of the world. My hands were shaking and my eyes were watering. I had never felt so much happiness in my whole life. For one time I was finally proud of myself.

"Don't let us down kid" the man said, with a smile on his face.

"I won't."

I exited the room and began to run towards the elevators. I felt so happy that I just wanted to scream. The elevator opened and I ran in it, without even looking first. When I felt the grip of someone's hands around my arm, I looked up and saw the person I thought I would never see again.

"You like to bump into people, don't you?" he laughed, letting me go and stepping aside, so I could stand next to him.

"I'm really sorry, I was so excited to go down to my family that I didn't even see if there was someone in the elevator." I said, laughing nervously.

"Let me guess, your audition went well?"

"Yes, I got three yeses."

"I bet I know who didn't give you a yes. It was Brad Wilson, the guy on the far left, wasn't it?"

"How do you know?"

"He is known for only giving one yes each year." He spoke

"That's something I should probably expect from a guy like him."

"Yes, it is."

The Elevator doors opened and we both walked out.

"How was your audition by the way?" I asked nicely.

"Stressful, I arrived one minute late and Brad wanted me to leave. Sabrina though, was nice enough to tell me to perform. I left with three yeses. Obviously the only one that said no was..."

"...Brad" I said, interrupting him

"Exactly" He smiled.

He had one of the prettiest smiles I had ever seen. I would have wanted to spend my entire day here with him and talk but I had to go tell my mom and my sister about my audition.

"I'm really sorry but I have to go find my mom and my sister. It was nice seeing you again." I spoke.

"Yeah, I have to go find my family too, have a nice day, see you in the first round of the show" he said, smiling.

"See you there" I responded.

I started running towards the waiting room. The hallways in this building looked all the same. That's when I finally found them. I

14

saw my sister Maya sitting next to my mom through the glass of the waiting room.

"Mom! I did it!" I screamed, making them turn around.

They got up from their seats and made their way out of the room. I started running faster towards them. This was the moment that brought me the most satisfaction. All the nights I've spend practicing for this day, all the stress with school and singing was finally worth it. I made my family proud, which was the most important thing for me. I felt my mom hugging me on one side and my sister on the other. This was the best moment of the whole audition.

"We're so proud of you darling.", said my mom.

"Yes! We are. I knew you could do it." Maya was rarely nice to me so I knew she was honest.

The ride home was very cool. We stopped at Mc Donald's to celebrate my successful audition. When we got home, I went to the bathroom to take a shower. This day had been exhausting. The audition worried me for weeks and now the whole stress was finally over. Today was really the best day of my life. There's also one more thing about today that I could never forget. His eyes. Those beautiful green eyes. He was genuinely the most beautiful person I've ever seen. Maybe It's stupid to think like this but I feel like it wasn't a coincidence that we met again in the elevator. I can't wait to see him again at the beginning of the first round of the competition.

Chapter three

This morning I woke up to my two little sisters jumping on my bed. They are twins. Their names are Lily and Robin.

"Mommy said you are going to take us to the park!" Lily looked up at me, knowing she could get anything with the puppy eyes she was making.

I got up from my bed and grabbed my backpack with a few things the twins need and my favourite book.

"Go downstairs. When I'm ready I'll take you"

"Thanks Caleb, we love you" Lily and Robin headed downstairs while I went to the bathroom to take a shower. After a short, cold shower, I stared into the mirror. My hair was messy and my skin looked pale. The eyebags under my eyes were showing how little sleep I had gotten. I was spending all my nights worrying about the next weekend, when the competition would start. I got out of the bathroom and headed downstairs to take the girls to the Park. When we arrived there, they let go off my hand and went to play on the slide. It was a sunny afternoon. I sat on a bench and started reading a book. My eyes were going from the twins and back to my book for about 40 minutes. It was starting to be late so I called the twins and we started to head back to the house. We were walking on a tiny pathway between the Park and the street, when a man approached us.

"Hey, you are one of the new guys that got cast for London-Talents!" I tall man with blonde hair and brown eyes was staring down at me.

"Yeah I am." I replied nicely.

"It's so nice to meet you. I was hoping to meet some concurrent before the show begins. I'm Nick Kytson, one of the crewmembers. I coordinate the lights on stage. I know from the last years that some concurrent are really nervous so if there's anything I can do for you, just let me know. "he said.

"Actually, I have a question. Is it true that Brad Wilson only gives one yes each year?" I asked.

"That is indeed true. There has never been a year where he gave more than just one yes. The person who gets his yes is usually pretty advantaged because they are liked by Brad. There's one advice that you'll for sure need. Don't get on his bad side. He is the inventor of this show and also one of the judges so he has the power over anything. If he doesn't like you, there's no chance you can win this competition." He spoke.

"There's a big probability that he already doesn't like me. I arrived late to the audition. "

"I think you'll be fine, as long as you try to agree with everything he says."

"Thank you for the advice Nick. Me and my sisters have to go now, see you next week."

"See you around" he said, before turning around and heading to the park

Lily and Robin were each holding one of my hands as we made our way home. When we entered the house, there was a pizza on the table waiting for us. We had dinner together and I put them to bed around 9. Then I went to my room and scrolled down the LondonTalents page on my computer. There were the pictured I had sent them for my audition and the pictures of everyone else. I scrolled a bit until I found what I was really looking for. Reeve Edward, 18 years old, lives in Holmes Chapel, United Kingdom. How was he able to look that good even on a picture sent for an audition? Everything about that picture was perfect. The way his brown locks stayed and the top of his head in a perfect way, how his eyes looked like the rainforest and how his smile was one of the most beautiful things I had ever seen in his live. The only thing that made me more nervous than staring the show, was seeing Edward. It had already gotten 11 so I closed my laptop and put on my pyjama. I went to the bathroom to brush my teeth and apply a hydrating cream to my face. I didn't feel really tired yet, so I decided to read a few chapters of one of my favorite books. The protagonist falls in love with someone she's not supposed to love, which makes her get hated from her family and everyone that she knows. This story really shows how sick people's minds can be, blaming a girl for who she falls in love with is wrong. We can't control our feelings. I decide to put down the book and try to

18

think of something else, or I would get mad at society for what they make people think is normal and what is wrong. My thoughts were wandering from the nice guy I met this afternoon, to the show that was staring in a week and to Edward, the beautiful green-eyed boy I couldn't wait to see again.

Chapter Four

This was the morning of the first round of LondonTalents. I woke up feeling really tired since I wasn't able to sleep for a long time. The evening before, I had planned my outfit for the day. It had to be special since the whole UK would see me on tv. But it had to be even more special because I will see Edward again. It's impossible to describe how much I missed seeing those beautiful green eyes. I didn't really know much about him, but I felt a connection that I hadn't felt in a long time. I turned around to look at my clock and saw that it was 5 in the morning. I had 30 minutes to get ready and to leave the house. My train ride is going to be two hours long. The first round will start at 9AM and I want to be sure to be there in time. I grabbed my yellow sweatshirts and my cross necklace. I put my black skinny jeans on and went to the bathroom to brush my teeth and wash my face. I tried to put a bit of hair gel in my hair to make them look less messy. While putting on my sweater and necklace, I went to grab the rings on my desk. They all had a really important meaning to me. One of them was my great great grandpa's ring, that was passed from generation to generation. It was a beautiful gold wedding ring with the initials of my great great grandpa, L.B. I put it on and grabbed my backpack with the essentials for the train ride. It was 5:25 when I went to my mom's room to tell her that I was leaving.

"Good luck sweetheart, I'm sure you'll do great." she said in a sleepy voice.

"Thank you, mom, see you tomorrow."

I left the room and went downstairs, where I grabbed a banana and left the house. When I arrived at the train station. I had to wait 10 minutes. My train arrived 1 minute early, which is weird here in Doncaster. I entered the train and sat into the seat next to the window. My earbuds were tangled in a bit not and it took me about 5 minutes to open them. When I had finally untangled my earbuds, a girl sat next to me on the train.

"Hi." She said quietly.

"Hi." I replied. She had short red hair and bright blue eyes. Her glasses were fitted on her tiny nose. She grabbed a book and started reading. I was curious and wanted to find out, what book she was reading.

"Hey, I'm sorry to bother, I just wanted to ask you what book you're reading." I spoke.

"No worries, I'm reading Harry Potter and the Half Blood Prince, it's actually the third time I'm reading it." She laughed.

"I love the Harry Potter books, who's your favorite character?" I asked

"Probably ginny, I relate to her. I too, have a lot of siblings and red hair." She giggled.

So, we talked for the next few hours. We talked about Harry Potter, about our favourite TV shows, about our schools and about ourselves.

"I just realized; I don't know your name." I spoke

"It's Darcy Wilson." She replied.

"My name is Caleb Brooks."

We continue to talk until we had reached the train station where I had to get out.

"I have to go now." I said.

"I have to go out too, we could walk together. Where are you going?" she asked

"To the Londontalents studios, I'm one of the concurrent this year." I spoke.

"I didn't know that, I'm one of the Judges' daughter." She replied. That's when I realised, this whole time, I was talking to Brad Wilson's daughter. She looked nothing like him and she was way nicer. We walked together until we arrived to the Studios. The big sign next to the entrance showed the four Judges, Brad Wilson, Oliver Johnson, Daniel Thomas and Sabrina Denot. We walked inside and she headed to the backstage after giving me a goodbye hug. I walked towards the waiting room. In an email I had gotten three days ago, they wrote that they would get me from the waiting room when it was my turn to perform. I sat in the chair and listened to the song I was going to perform for a few times. When I looked up, there were a lot of people in the room, but only one person caught my eyes instantly. He looked up too and I finally got to see those beautiful green eyes again.

Chapter five

---------------------------The first round------------------------

There he was, right in front of me. This was the moment I've waited for, the moment I was so freighted about and the moment that filled all my thoughts for the past weeks. And now there he was. The green tight sweater that he was wearing made his emerald eyes shine like the sun on a summer day of august. His spiral shaped hair was sitting perfectly on his shoulder. For all these weeks the thought of seeing him again made my knees weak. I had planned what I wanted to say when I finally saw him again, but now that he was here, standing in front of me, I had lost my voice.

"Hi, how are you?" I coughed and felt my throat tightened after the words I spoke.

"I'm really good, it's nice to see you again." He replied.

I put my hand in my hair trying to take the attention away from my face, that was clearly blushing really hard.

"It's nice to see you too." I smiled.

"So, are you exited to start the competition?" he pushed the curl that fell in front of his eyes back behind his ears.

"To be honest I'm a little nervous. Do you already know what song you're going to sing for the first round?"

"Yes, I do, I will sing I just called to say I love you by Stevie Wonder. I chose it because I sang Isn't she lovely for my audition and I

24

feel like my voice fits with his songs. Do you already know what you're going to sing?"

"I will sing Someone like you by Adele."

"I love that song! I'm sure you will be great." He responded.

He walked back to his chair and pulled out his phone. After a few minutes, a tall guy in a black suit entered the waiting room.

"Caleb Brooks, it's time for your performance." he said.

I stood up from my chair and walked towards the glass door, separating the waiting room from the hallway. The security guy turned around and started to walk out of the room, so I followed him. Just as I was about to leave, I felt someone grab my arm.

"Good luck, I'm sure you'll be amazing."

Edward smiled at me as I nodded in response. I followed the man until we arrived to the right part of the stage. The staff had already given me a microphone. The host of Londontalents, Calum Roberts, came up to me to tell me that I will be performing in two minutes.

"Hey Caleb, good luck!" I heard a man say.

When I turned around, I saw Nick, the light coordinator that I had met at the park.

"Hi Nick, how are you?"

"I'm good and I'm so excited for the show, are you nervous?" he asked kindly.

"A little bit to be honest but I think that's normal." I replied.

"I'm sure you'll be fantastic."

"Caleb, you're up in 20 seconds." Calum had come back to tell me to be ready.

"Well, see you after your performance." Said Nick.

"See you later" I replied.

I heard Calum countdown from five. When he arrived at one he gave me a little push towards the stage. When I got out on stage, the lights were focused on my and I almost couldn't see the crowd. After a few seconds, the lights got weaker and I could see the thousands of people looking at me. The judges were sitting at the front. I walked towards the middle of the enormous stage. It was my first time ever performing in front of such a big crowd. I had been in a few musicals in Highschool but I was never the only one singing. All of the people that were sitting in this theatre were looking at me. When I arrived at the center of the stage, I lifted my microphone to speak.

"Hi I'm Caleb Brooks and I will perform Someone like you by Adele."

Sabrina Denot, one of the Judges, nodded and smiled at me. I sat down at the white piano that was brought in. When I placed my fingers on the piano and started playing, I closed my eyes and hoped it would all go well.

Chapter six

My first round went great. After I was done singing, everyone stood up and clapped for me. Even Brad Wilson clapped for a few seconds. They told me I was really great and that they would see me later during the pairing phase. In the pairing phase you basically get put in a group with another singer and you have to perform a duet. That phase will start in one hour so I still had time to go grab something to eat from the cafeteria. When I arrived there, I saw Darcy sitting alone, so I went and joined her.

"Hi Darcy." I greeted her.

"Hey Caleb, I saw your performance, it was really great." she said.

"Thank you, what did you do this whole time?" I asked

"I only come here because my dad works here. I spent this whole time either watching performances or listening to music in the outdoor area. It's actually really great. There's a fountain and a nice little garden. Do you want to go there?"

"That would be great, I really need some fresh air."

We walked to the outdoor area and sat on a bench. Darcy pulled her hair behind and put it in a low ponytail. She then grabbed a pack of cigarettes and a lighter from her pocket.

"Do you want one?" she asked.

I shook my head, since I don't smoke, and rested my back on the bench.

"Does your dad know that you smoke? He looks really strict."

27

"He doesn't, but he still has other reasons to make my life hard and remind me that I'm the family disappointment. Ever since he met my girlfriend and found out I'm bi, he makes me pray every day because apparently being bi is a sin." she said.

"I didn't know you had a girlfriend, what is she like?" I replied, trying to take her mind off her dad and to make her think of someone she loves.

"She's the most wonderful person ever. Her name is Elizabeth, but everyone calls her Liz." she giggled. "She is the most caring person I have ever met. When no one in my family was here for me, she was there to help me. I really don't know what I did to deserve her."

"She sounds lovely." I replied.

Just after I said that, the speakers announced that all the participants had to meet in the big dance hall to be put in duos. Me and Darcy headed to the dance room after she finished her cigarette. When we arrived, most of the contestants were there already. I had to sit in a row with 5 other contestants and Darcy stood in the corner of the room, where she wouldn't be recorded by the cameras. I saw the host of the show walking in the room with three cameras pointed at him so I figured that the show had started.

"Dear spectators, we are here in the dancing room to sort these contestants in duos. They will each have a week to practice their duet and perform in Saturday night live, here on Londonstalents. Now I'll give the word to the judges"

28

The cameras slowly turned towards the big Table in the middle of the room. Oliver Johnson, one of the Judges, leaned forward to his microphone and said: "Hello contestants on Londonstalents, you are all entering the duo phase of the competition. After you perform with your partner, you will be able to decide if you want to stay a duo for the rest of the competition, or if one of you will have to leave right away. Let's start with the first duo. Thomas Clarke and Page Collings please step forward."

A tall girl with long black hair stood up, a few rows in front of me. The guy was sitting right behind me. He was a really handsome guy with a defined facial structure and blonde wavy hair. The both stood in front of the Judges.

"You are a duo now, good luck."

They walked out of the room together. For the next few minutes, the judges continued to call people up and put them in pairs. I was a bit nervous to find out who my partner will be because I didn't want to have to work with someone I don't like. Finally, I heard the judge call my name.

"Caleb Brooks and Edward Reeve please step to the front."

I had just won the fucking lottery.

"You are now a duo, good luck."

As we were walking out of the room, Edward leaned towards me and whispered; "Wouldn't have wanted to work with anyone else." He gave me a little smirk as we left the room. We walked towards the cafeteria that was right next to the dance room. One table for two was still free so we sat there.

"I'm really happy that I'll get to work with you." I spoke.

"I'm really happy too, we should go on a date tonight, just to plan our performance obviously." He gave me another smirk.

I smiled more than I had planned to do. Gently, I nodded in response.

"I will wait for you here at the cafeteria tonight at eight o clock if that's alright to you." he said.

"Can't wait."

He stood up from the chair and walked out of the cafeteria. My heart felt like I had just finished running a marathon. It was beating fast then I had ever heard it beat. I got up and started to walk towards the exit of the theatre. With all my stuff in my backpack, I took the next train and went home. When I entered the door, I heard my little sisters running towards the stairs. They jumped in my arms and hugged me. Being away for them is really hard because they mean the world to me and I love spending time with them. My mom was still in the kitchen, smiling at me. I hugged her too and told her a bit about my experience at the theatre today. She told me she had seen my performance and thought it was amazing. When I told her, I was going on a date tonight, she seemed sort of surprised. I was always really shy and didn't have a lot of friends, so it was a surprise to her, that I had managed to get a date with someone. I was meeting Edward at 8, which with

30

a 30 minutes car ride and a stop to get flowers, would leave me with one hour to shower, dry my hair, pick something to wear and brush my teeth. I ran up the stairs towards my room. The floor was a mess, since I hadn't cleaned it up this morning. I went into the shower and washed my hair. After, I dried my hair and brushed my teeth. When I got back into my room, I picked up my black jeans from the ground and put them on. I grabbed a white shirt and my red flannel out of the closet and put those on too. My keys were laying on top of a big pile of clothes. I picked them up and went downstairs. My mother gave me a goodbye kiss and opened the front door for me, wishing me good luck on my date. I got into my car, turned on the radio, and got on the way to the flower shop. The old lady that worked there was always really nice to me, when I picked flowers. When I walked in the shop, she gave me a worried look. Every time I had entered the shop before, I was buying flowers for a funeral, so I had to reassure her that nobody died. When I told her, I was actually going on a date, she smiled and helped me pick out the most beautiful flowers in the shop. After paying, I got back into my car and went to the Londontalents studios, where I was supposed to meet Edward. The doors were still open for people that wanted to rehears in the theatre rooms. Edward was standing in front of the cafeteria. He was wearing a brown hoodie and some jeans. His long curls were put in a man bun. I walked towards him, trying to contain a smile.

"Wow, you look stunning." He turned around and smiled after seeing me.

"You don't look bad yourself." He answered.

"I brought you these, I hope you like them." I gave him the daisies I had bought.

"Thank you so much, I love them." He had a huge smile on his face.

"So, where should we go?" I ask, wondering what he had planned for this date. That's when I noticed a basket behind him. It had all kinds on food and drinks inside of it.

"We're doing a picnic." he said.

We walked out of the theatre and crossed the street, going towards one of London's most famous parks. It's known for the beautiful flowers and the wonderful animals living there. We found a spot right under the moonlight. Edward took a table cloth out of the basket and put it on the ground. We sat on it and started to unpack a few of the thing that were in the basket.

"Do you know what I realised? We are on a date and are going to perform live tomorrow but I don't actually know anything about you." I spoke. Edward gave a sidewards glance and giggled.

"Ask me anything and I'll respond." He answered.

"Tell me something about your childhood." He reacted really surprised.

"That's not what I thought you would ask me but here it goes. I was born on February 1st. My mom died when I was born due to

32

complications. Since I was a little kid, my dad didn't want anything to do with me. I suppose he was mad about what happened to my mom and blamed it on me. He left me in front of a hospital and the nurses found me and brought me to an orphanage. The first "parents" that I had were really abusive. They always said I was a really beautiful child and I was going to be a model someday, so they decided to not make me eat enough, so I could stay skinny. When social services found out, I got brought back to a new orphanage, where I met a lot of kids that were in similar situations like mine. When I was 5, I was sent to another family. They treated me very well and adopted me a few months later. They're my current family and I couldn't wish for anything better, but I still would like to meet my biological dad someday. Ah and, I almost forgot, when I was born, my name wasn't Edward, it was Harry. My parents changed it after adopting me, because they didn't like the name Harry. Now, tell me something about your childhood."

I was shocked, in tears almost. My mouth was wide open and I was trying to process the information that I had just been told. From the way he said it so calmly, I assume it wasn't so bad for him to tell this story.

"I'm sorry for what you went through, my father abandoned me too. When my sister Maya was born, he decided that he wanted a new start somewhere else, so he left. I was only two years old, I don't remember it, but I hate him for how he made my mother

33

feel. Two years ago, he randomly showed up at out house. He said he wanted to apologize and that he had been an idiot for leaving. He wanted to get to know his kids and spend time with them. My mother was really mad about him thinking he can just come back into our lives like that. My two younger sisters, Robin and Lily, are actually just my stepsisters. He got mad when he found out my mom had moved on and he tried to get in the house, but my mom called the cops and filed a restraining order against him. I haven't seen him since. But you know, my childhood was cool, I guess." I left out a giggle after that last sentence, since it wasn't really appropriate to the situation. Edward looked my in the eyes, held my hand and pulled me into a hug. I tried to laugh about my situation and he still understood how hurt I was deep inside. He put his problems by the side and hugged me. No one had ever hugged me like that. His hands were gently running through my hair. We slowly pulled away from the hug.

He smiled and said: "I think I know what song we could perform tomorrow."

Chapter seven

Yesterday night, I brought Edward back home and went home myself. We talked a lot and I had a lot of fun. I think I'm really starting to fall for him. The way he hugged me yesterday, the way he talks, the way he slowly runs his hand through his hair and fixes his crazy, beautiful locks. Everything about him makes me realize how much I'm starting to like him. It was already 8am, I got up, put on a pair of jeans and a black hoodie, and went to brush my teeth. My hair looked surprisingly good this morning, so I didn't have to fix it. My mom had packed me my breakfast to eat on the way to the theatre. She knew I would be late and I wouldn't have any time to eat breakfast at home. I grabbed it and sprinted out of the house. I decided that I was going to go with my car instead of the train. My flannel was still in the car because I took it off yesterday and forgot to bring it to my room. I started the engine and drove off. When I passed the train station, I saw Darcy sitting on a bench, waiting for the train. I stopped my car and called her over.

"Darcy, if you want a ride to the theatre, I can take you. "I shouted. She turned around, saw my car and started running towards me.

"Hey, you're a life saver, I missed the last train and I would have been late if it weren't for you." She gets in the car and we drive off.

"So, what's up with you and curly boy? And don't try to tell me there's nothing going on, I saw your face when you got put in a team with him." She smirks and pushes me with her elbow.

"Alright, we met at the audition day, bumped into each other two times. Literally bumped, like falling on the floor type of bumping. In the waiting room, we saw each other again and talked before I went to do my performance. We got put together into a group for round two and he asked me out on a date. He brought food and drinks and we did a picnic in the grass, talked about our childhood, laughed and ate together and then I accompanied him back home. I'm not sure about what I'm feeling for him and I hope I'll figure it out soon."

Her mouth had dropped. "You are in love! That's so cute oh my god. And he asked you on a date? He likes you too! You guys are so cute."

"I'm not in love….and he was just being nice."

"You know, I don't ask people out on dates just to be nice and I'm sure you don't do it either. So yes, he does like you. I can't wait to see you guys perform later. Did you choose a song yet?"

"We did. It was his idea and we couldn't stop laughing after he told me what the song was. I'm not going to tell you the name, just know, we talked about our shitty father and childhoods before deciding the name. Trust me, when you'll hear it, you will die laughing."

We had almost arrived at the theatre, I dropped Darcy off at the V.I.P entrance and went to park my car. A lot of the people outside of the theatre were standing in groups of two, probably practicing their performance. Me and Edward just discussed what song we were going to sing and who will sing what part, I had never heard him sing. He had watched my performance, so he knew what I sounded like, but I had never heard him sing. The entrance for the contestants was starting to get crowded with the pair wanting to enter the theatre. I sprinted inside and started to look for Edward. Once I spotted him, I walked towards him. He wasn't really hard to notice, since he was wearing a bright green sweater with a dog and the words 'Stay away from toxic people' printed on the front. I really liked his sense of style. He saw me and waved at me.

"Hey, are you exited for out performance?" he asked.

"I am. I'm also really nervous."

"Don't be. We will give it our best and see how it goes. I was thinking that while we wait for our time to perform, which will be in an hour, do you want to grab a coffee and walk to the garden?"

"That would be nice." We walked to the cafeteria and ordered. I chose a cappuccino and he wanted a latte macchiato. When I was about to get my wallet from my pocket, he stopped my hand and said: "Don't worry about it, it's on me." Our orders were done really fast, we took them and walked to the door that led to the garden. Next to the door, I saw Darcy talking to a girl, a beautiful girl, which I suppose, was her girlfriend. We walked up to them to say hi.

"Well, hello there, is this dreamy boy you were talking about this whole morning?" Darcy winked at me and I felt myself blush. This was such an embarrassing situation. Why would she call him dreamy boy when he's standing right in front of her? I looked over to Edward, that was just looking down and smiling. Darcy faced me again and mouthed the words 'He likes you'.

"You must be the gorgeous girlfriend of Darcy's, right?" I asked the girl next to her.

"I am," she laughed "And you must be the lifesaver that brought her here this morning." We both laughed.

"Edward, this is Darcy, Brad Wilson's daughter, but don't worry, she's nice."

Edward leaned his arm towards Darcy.

"I'm Edward, but I'm sure you already knew that seen the circumstances and the cute nickname." He turned towards me. "Dreamy boy, is that what you call me? Well, I'm flattered."

I giggled at his statement and started to blush again.

"We have to go now, we were thinking about sitting in the garden before having to perform, bye girls, see you later." They said goodbye and went towards the cafeteria. Me and Edward went to the garden and sat on a bench. We talked about how we wanted to perform the song and about how exited we were to perform together.

"Now that we talked about all this stuff, I want to get to know you a little better, you know, the basics. So, what's your favorite color?"

"It was red a few weeks ago, but now it's definitely emerald green." I really hoped Edward understood the connection of the color and his eyes. He blushed so I think he did understand it. "What's your favorite color?"

"Blue, not any shade of blue, it has to be louis blue, like your eyes." I didn't expect him to be so directed with his compliments, so it surprised me at first, but then I smiled and felt my face become red.

"What's your favorite band?" I asked him.

"I really like Queen, especially Freddie Mercury. I think he had an incredible sense of style and a lightful personality on stage. I often try to take inspiration from him for my outfits and I would love to be like him when I perform, to have his confidence."

"I think your style is very cool and I'm sure you'll be able to reach that type of confidence on stage someday."

"Thank you, Caleb."

I saw that he was about to ask something, but the speaker called our names and we had to go and get ready for our performance. I headed towards the right side of the backstage and Edward went to the left side. The crew set me up with a microphone and told me to wait until the stage was completely empty and the lights were low. Edward was on the other side and I could see him cracking his knuckles and trying to calm himself down. I showed him a thumbs up when he looked towards me, to let him know that we'll be alright. The stage light turned dark and the crew members told me to get on stage. On the other side, they were saying the same to Edward. We both walked to the middle of the stage and were flashed by the bright lights.

"Good evening Edward Reeve and Caleb Brook, what are you going to perform for us." Brad Wilson welcomed us and gave us a dirty look right after. Edward put his microphone text to his lips, those beautiful lips, and said: "Hello Judges, hello audience, we will be performing a song to which me and Caleb both relate to and that we both like. It's by The Neighbourhood and it's called Daddy Issues."

The crowd applauded and the Judges wished us good luck. My eyes met Edward's when the beat of the song started to play. It's a slow beat and I see Edward's eyes close as he prepares to sing the first line.

"Take…. you…. like…. a……drug"

His Voice was fucking beautiful. It was a deep voice and he sang those first words with a type of voice that sent shivers down my spine and butterflies in my stomach. The next line was mine. I kept my eyes open and watched Edward in his, which he had opened again after the line.

40

"I…. taste…you…on…my…tongue."

Edward gave me a smirk which made me unfocused from the song for a moment, but I was ready to sing the next part together.

"You ask me what I'm thinking about…..I tell you that I'm thinking about…..Whatever you're thinking about…….Tell me something that I'll forget……..And you might have to tell me again……It's crazy what you'll do for a friend."

Our voices harmonize perfectly and everyone in that theatre could hear it. They were a perfect match for each other, like two pieces of a puzzle, a beautiful puzzle that everyone would love and would find amazing. A loud applause came from the crowd. We finished the performance beautifully.

"I'd run away and hide with you…...I know that you got daddy issues, and I do too"

It felt like the crowd exploded with cheers, applauses and scream. All of the Judges were standing, even Brad. I would have loved to look at the crowd, at every person in there and see how they were cheering for us, but the only person I could look at was Edward. He has a massive smile on his face. In that moment I realised, I had reached the peak of my existence.

Chapter Eight

----------------------------Family time----------------------------

The audience was still clapping for us, I grabbed Edwards's hand and pulled him down to bow in front of everyone. When we got up, I put my arm over his shoulder and hugged him for what felt like years. My face was squeezed into his shoulder, I couldn't stop smiling. We pulled apart, realising the Judges wanted to move on to the votes.

"Wow! You guys were fantastic, the way your voices harmonized together, I'm sure everyone could feel a special connection between you guys tonight. For me it's an absolute yes." The audience cheered at Sabrina's vote. Oliver Johnson brought his microphone closer and said: "I have to agree with Sabrina, you guys have an incredible voice together and you're a perfect fit for each other. It's a yes from me." The audience bust into another loud cheer. Everyone went quiet when it was time for Brad to speak.

"I think you guys have potential; you just don't know how to use it. Awful song choice, not enough harmonizing and your presence on stage is just not enough. It's a no for me." The audience booed at Brad. Edward grabbed my hand and squeezed it tight, to tell me that everything would be okay. If Daniel Thomas, the last Judge, would agree with Brad, me and Edward would have two no, which would mean we get eliminated.

"I usually agree with what Brad says. This time, I have to admit, you guys were incredible. The song choice is questionable, but it

fits your voices very well. It's a yes for me."
I turned towards Edward and, without thinking twice, I jumped into his arms. He lifted me up and hugged me, while we hear the loud screams of the people in the crowd, almost as happy as us.

"Before we let you go, we have to ask the important question. Do you guys want to part ways again and find your success in solo careers or do you guys want to stay a duo for the rest of the competition?"

That's when I realised, that me and Edward had never even talked about this. We came here to get a career as solo artists and I never thought about being in a duo. What if it won't work out? What if this performance was good and the rest of them will be bad? What if Edward wants to continue as a solo artist? I look towards him, noticing that he my same look, a worried look. Suddenly, he grabbed my hand, pulled me closer and whispered: "I like spending time with you, we should stay as a duo." He backs off again and I nod.

"We're going to stay as a duo." The crowd applauded again, which made me think that they wanted us to stay a duo too. We walk off the stage, leaving behind an incredible feeling of happiness. We walked out of the backstage and towards the cafeteria. Nick was running towards us, on his way to the backstage.

"You guys were amazing, I'm in a big hurry but it was fantastic, you're for sure my favorite duo on the show." Before we could say anything to thank him, he ran off towards the backstage. We walked to the cafeteria to have something to eat. I took a salad and Edward chose a chicken sandwich. We sat at one of the tables in the back of the cafeteria.

"You have a beautiful voice," I said.

"You too, maybe it's just me but I felt like our souls connected when we were singing. I'm happy that I will end this journey with you." I smiled at him, trying to contain an even bigger smile that would have given away too much. We finished eating and said goodbye. I went into my car and drove all the way home. While I was driving, I thought about our performance again. The way he closed his eyes while singing and the way the words left his mouth so delicately. How he grabbed my hand when we were about to find out if we would stay or not. How he hugged he back when I jumped on him and how I just felt his happiness without him having to say anything. I grabbed my phone and called Darcy. My phone connected to the car speaker and Darcy picked up.

"Hey Caleb, I saw the performance, you were right, when I heard the song, I started laughing because it makes so much sense. You guys were incredible, really. When you jumped on him, I let out a scream because you guys are so cute. How do you feel?"

"You were right, about the whole feelings thing. I feel something for Edward, ever since we bumped into each other at the auditions. He makes my heart skip a beat every time he talks or looks at me. I feel like I should tell him but I'm afraid that he doesn't feel the same way."

44

"Are you kidding me? How did you not see how he looked at you during the performance? The smirks, the laughs, everything. Trust me, I know when someone is attracted to someone and he is. Those looks he gave you are not friendship looks, so stop being so scared and confess your feelings already, you don't have forever."

"I will, I just need to wait for the right moment."

"There might not be a right moment, just go for it."

"I'll try to take your advice, I really will, I'm home now, I'll see you tomorrow."

"See ya."

My family was not home when I arrived. At first it scared me, but then I remembered that they had a dinner planned with the neighbours. I didn't feel like going so I just went upstairs and took a shower. After I was done, I laid on my bed and started reading. I loved to read, it brought me into a reality were everyone was happy and everything was perfect. It made me forget about my own problems for a bit. But now, for the first time ever, I didn't have any problems to forget. My life was going well for the first time. I sat there on my bed, reading about two people, so madly in love, but they never had a chance to tell one another. That's when it hit me. Darcy is right. I have to tell Edward how I feel, as soon as possible. I can't go over to his house tonight, since I haven't spent any time with my family in this last days and I miss them a lot. Tomorrow, the day of the finale, I will tell him. I will stand in front of him and tell him how I feel. I will tell him how he makes me feel. But for now, I sink my head back into my book, imagining how these characters must have felt after not confessing their love, and knowing, I won't have to feel that way. I heard the front door open, so I went downstairs and hugged the twins, that were coming back home with Maya and my mom.

"How was dinner?" I asked.

"Great, how was your date yesterday? You came home late and left early this morning." My mom took off her jacket and sat down at the dining table, telling me to sit down text to her and tell her everything that happened.

"We went on a picnic date in the park, talked a bit and then I drove him home."

"I saw you guys perform today. You were really good, I'm glad you stayed a duo."

"Yeah, me too, do you guys want to watch a movie together tonight?" My little sisters jumped on the couch yelling: "Yes mommy, please let us watch a movie tonight."

"That's fine with me. Ask Maya if she wants to watch it with us." I got up the stairs to maya's room and knocked on the door. Her room was one of those typical teenage girl's room. She was obsessed with a famous boyband, she even had cardboard cut-outs of her favorite member, which I found kind of creepy. But otherwise, it was a cute room.

"Do you want to watch a movie with us?"

46

"Yes, I'll be there in a minute."

We all sat on a couch and watched Back to the future. I suggested that we watch the first one, since it's way more interesting that the other two. I've always had a crush on Marty McFly, it was probably the way he dressed, I seem to notice that a lot in people. When the movie ended, we all went to bed, waiting for tomorrow, the day of the finale.

Chapter nine

----------------------------The finale----------------------------

I woke up at 9am, because I had to get ready and go pick up Edward, so we could practice for tonight. We were one of the last five groups left. There was us, two girls and the rest were solo. I showered and packed my stuff. I put on sweatpants and a hoodie, so I would feel more comfortable to rehearsal. I had prepared my suit that I would wear during the finale. I went into my car and put all my stuff inside it. Then I got back into the house and ate breakfast with my family.

"We're going to be there tonight; I already bought the tickets. I hope you'll spot us in the crowd."

"Thank you for coming."

"I would never miss it. One thing I wanted to tell you before you go is, whatever happens tonight, I'm incredibly proud of you and all of your sisters are too." We hugged and they all accompanied me to my car. I got inside and waved to them one last time before leaving. Edward's house was only twenty minutes away from mine. All the channels of the radio were talking about the finale of tonight. Me and Edward will have to choose a song this afternoon, since we didn't have time to choose it sooner. I pulled up to his house and texted him to tell him that I had arrived. He got out of the house wearing some sweats and a hoodie, just like me, and with a plastic bag with his suit in it. We packed his stuff into my car.

"Hi Edward, feeling nervous?" I asked.

"Not yet, I'll probably feel nervous when we're about to perform."

"Yeah, me too."

He got in the car and we drove off his driveway. His mom was standing outside of the house, waving to Edward. She was a beautiful woman with long, dark hair. Edward waved back at her and turned over to me. "Did you hear all the radios talking about the finale? It feels like the whole world will be watching us perform. Do you have any idea of what we could perform tonight?"

"I'm not sure yet. We can look through our playlists when we get there and see if there's something we both like."

"Sounds good to me."

He turned toward the window and took a picture of the sun.

"Do you like taking pictures?" I asked.

"It's one of the few things I'm good at. I like singing and photography, they let me express myself in different ways. My Instagram is full of pictures of everywhere I go. I could just go to a simple gas station, see something that I think looks good, take a picture of it and upload it to my Instagram. Can I take a picture of you driving? You look really cute." I giggled and nodded. He took a picture of me and showed me the result.

"Wow, you look fantastic."

"You just take good pictures. I don't usually look good in pictures." We laughed together and talked about things we like to do for the whole car ride. It was 11am when we arrived at the theatre. The doors for the contestant are open and we get inside. There's a rehears room where you can practice the performance. We get to the room, close the door behind us and sit on the floor. "Let me see your playlist for some ideas." Edward takes my phone and scrolls through my Spotify playlists. "Would you prefer something slow and sweet or something fast and rocky?" "Slow and sweet, it fits our voices more." He continues to scroll down for a while, apparently not finding the perfect song for a finale. Suddenly he stops scrolling and hands me over the phone.

"I think this would be perfect with your vocals and our harmonizing skills." He had chosen one of my favorite songs. The song talks about a relationship which is not socially accepted. They have to hide their relationship and can't be seen in public together.

"I love this song, It's perfect."

We practised for a few hours, trying very hard to hit every sing note in that song. This was the most important performance of our lives. Winning would mean going home with 500k each and a contract to produce music with the four best artists in the world.

"Do you prefer if we keep the performance simple or do you want to add a choreography?" I am not good at dancing, the idea of having to dance in front of practically the whole world made me want to   throw   up.

"I think that without a choreography, we'll be freer and the performance will show our true selves even more.

50

"You're right, there is something I want to add to this performance though. We still have a few hours to announce what we need for our performance and I think I have a perfect idea." He talks for the next twenty minutes about the fantastic idea he had. Fantastic can't even begin to describe what he came up with. "I love it, go tell the crew members so they'll ger everything ready."

He got up and walked out of the room. I had never been in the rehears room before. It was really big, like a ballet room. It had a few seats and a tiny stage where everyone could practice their performance. I was still sitting on the floor, waiting for Edward to come back. Suddenly my phone started to vibrate. I looked at it and it was a call from an unknown number. I picked up my phone, answered and pulled it close to my ear: "Hi, who is this?" I asked. At first, there was no response but after a few seconds a deep voice said: "Hey kiddo, It's me, your father. I know you hate me and don't want to talk to me, but I just wanted to congratulate you for making it to the finale. You're getting really famous you know; everyone is talking about the finale. I will be watching you tonight and I really hope you and your friend win this competition." I was shocked. He was the last person I expected on the other side of this call. He abandoned me when I was young, he abused my mother the whole time they were together (I know that because my mom had to tell the whole story for the restraining order) and he never apologized for anything. He had a new family, a wife and two sons. I know it because I saw them at the park one day. He was playing soccer with them, like he should have been doing with me too. I never received a call for any birthdays, he never showed up to my soccer games or my musicals when I was little. Now that he hears my name on every radio, he finds the balls to call and congratulate.

"First of all, don't call me kiddo. Second, I don't want your congratulations on anything. Everything that I reached in life, was without you. You were never there for me. My first game of soccer, no. My first musical, no. The first time I rode a bike, no. When I got into my dream college, no. You were never here for me and now that you hear my name everywhere, you pick up the phone and call me? YOU COULD HAVE DONE THAT THE LAST 19 YEARS OF MY FUCKING LIFE. And yes, you're right, I hate you and I don't want anything to do with you or anyone in your perfect little family. I really hope you're being a good father to those kids, no one deserves to go through what me and Maya went through. Do you even remember Maya? I doubt it since you left a week after she was born. HOW CAN YOU LEAVE YOUR ONE WEEK YEAR OLD DAUGHTER? WHAT KIND OF MONSTER ARE YOU? I NEVER WANT TO HEAR YOUR VOICE AGAIN; I NEVER WANT TO SEE YOU AGAIN AND I NEVER WANT YOU TO EVER CALL ME AGAIN PRETEND-ING LIKE EVERYTHING IS OKAY BECAUSE IT'S NOT." I broke down in tears and hung up the phone. The whole conversation was too much. Right when I started crying, Edward walked back into the room, not noticing my tears at first. When he saw me on the ground, my face buried into my hands, crying, he ran towards me and held me. He pulled me into a hug without saying anything. He made me feel save, he was the only one that made me feel save. His hand was slowly rubbing my back, trying to console me. He didn't let me go until I had completely stopped crying. I pulled out of the hug and looked him in the eyes, kind of embarrassed that he had seen me cry.

"You're not alone Caleb." He wiped a tear off my cheek and pulled me into another hug, resting his chin on top of my head and slowly playing with my hair. When I could talk again, I told him what happened, I told him about my dad and about how mad it made me feel that he called. He still hadn't pulled away from the hug. "I know something that could make you feel better. I talked to the crew and they think my idea is really cool. We can go check it out if you want to. Or we can stay here, whatever you prefer."

"Let's go see it." We stood up from the ground and walked to the backstage to talk to the crew.

"Hi guys. Edward told me about the lightning idea you guys had, go on stage, I'll turn the lights on and you tell me if you like it." It was Nick, the guy I has met at the park. He turned back towards the commands of the lights. Me and Edward walked to the middle of the stage. On the ceiling, there were a dozen stage lights. Two of those turned on and were pointed, one on me and one on

Edward. He raised his hand and gave Nick a thumbs up to let him know that he could turn on the other lights too. They turned on and the whole theatre, every single seat in that room was a different color. They were aligned in a way that was forming a beautiful rainbow in the theatre.

"It looks beautiful, It's perfect for our song." Edward gave a thumbs up to Nick, so that he knew that everything was perfect. We walked off the stage and back into the rehears room, where we practiced out entrance and performance of tonight. It was getting late and the first people were starting to arrive. We got out clothes from the car and changed into our suits. I was expecting Edward to wear a basic, black suit, but no, he put on a light blue suit with flowers on the jacket, he looked gorgeous.

"Wow, I love your suit, I wish I would have worn something more special and not so basic."

"Actually, if you really want to, I have a green suit here too. I didn't know if I wanted to wear blue or green, so I brought both. I you want, you can wear the green one." He opened to plastic zip-up bag again and pulled out a beautiful green suit. The fabric was soft and beautifully ironed. He handed me over the suit and I put it on. I walked over to the mirror, that was usually used to practice dances and see how you were doing, and was shocked by the way this suit looked on me. It was the perfect fit, which was a bit weird, since Edward was a lot taller than me, but after he was so nice, I wasn't going to ask him if he really brought this for himself.

"It's beautiful, if you really don't mind, I would love wearing it tonight."

"It's perfect for you. You have to wear it, it'll be perfect." We both walked out of the rehearsal room and towards the backstage. On our way there, we saw Darcy and her girlfriend. Darcy was wearing a long, blue dress and her girlfriend had a short, red cocktail dress on.

"Okay wow you guys look fantastic." She hugged me and Edward.

"Thank you, Darcy, you both look really good too."

"Thank you, we'll be in the first row, cheering for you guys. I'm sure you'll win, you're the best duo in this competition."

"Thank you so much. We hope to win too. See you later." Edward said.

They walked towards their places. Me and Edward will be the third ones to perform. We wouldn't be able to watch the other performances from the audience, since we had to be prepared for our performance, so we just stayed in the backstage. We heard the opening music, which meant that the show had started and was live all over the world.

"Ladies and Gentleman, I, the host of Londontalents, am honoured to welcome you to the grand finale. The five groups performing today will be judged by you, watching at home. After all of the performances, you will have 10 minutes to go on our official site, Londontalents.com, and vote for your favorite performance. The winner will go home one million dollar and a contract with one of the best companies in the world. Are you ready?" The crowd cheered and applauded. The big screen light up and the name of the first duo appeared.

"Please welcome Jade and Jason, singing where have you been, by Rihanna" The music started and they walked up to the middle of the stage. Their microphones were not the ones you have to hold, which means they probably had a dance routine planned, which we had not. When the performance ended, the crowd exploded in applauses and screams. The contestants bowed down and got off the stage. In the finale, the Judges couldn't say anything until the end. After the winner is decided, they will choose who will get to manage them.

"The next contestant is the youngest one of this season. Please welcome, Nancy García, singing bad romance, by Lady Gaga."
The young girl walked up on stage and seemed very nervous. I couldn't focus on her performance because I knew, me and Edward would be next. It was the finale, the most important day of our lives, it had to go well. My whole family is sitting in the audience and I want to make them proud.

"Edward, I'm nervous, I really hope everything works out like we want it to."
He pulled me closer to him, grabbed my chin and looked me deep into my eyes.

"We'll be alright Caleb, don't worry, I'm by your side." I hugged him tight before letting him go and reminding him that he had to go to the other side of the backstage, so he would go on stage from one side and I would come out from the other. He walked off and I focused on the girl's performance again, which had almost ended. The crowd applauded, not as much as for the last performance though.

"The next contestants are the duo that was appreciated the most by the audience the last time. Ladies and gentleman, welcome Caleb and Edward, singing secret love song by Little mix."

The lights turned off on the stage. A few seconds later, every person in the audience was lighted by a colorful light, which formed a rainbow in the theatre. Edward walked out on the stage and started to sing, a white light pointed at him that followed him everywhere we went.

"When you hold me in the street and you kiss me on the dance floor."

I walked out on stage too, not so nervous anymore. This was our moment, our very special moment together and no price would change the fact that we were on this stage, together. Even if we're not going to win, I know that I had the best time singing with the boy I fell in love with.

"I wish that it could be like that. Why can't it be like that? 'Cause I'm yours"

We moved closer to the middle of the stage. Edward was happy, I could see it by the smile on his face. The lights that were following us finally met in the middle of the stage. He took my hand, held it to his chest and sang out the next line.

"We keep behind closed doors. Every time I see you, I die a little more. Stolen moments that we steal as the curtain falls. It'll never be enough"

I wanted to sing my next line with the most feelings I could put in it. I wanted Edward to understand how much I love him, how much he means to me.

"It's obvious you're meant for me. Every piece of you, it just fits perfectly. Every second, every thought, I'm in so deep. But I'll never show it on my face."

The solo parts were over, before we started to sing the chorus, I realized that there was a swing, covered in flowers, hanging from the ceiling. Edward took my hand and guided me towards the swing. We sat on it and it started to rise up. I realised it must have been a surprise planned by Edward. I think the audience realised it too, by seeing the surprised look on my face. While the swing was rising more, we sang the next part together.

"But we know this. We got a love that is homeless.

Why can't you hold me in the street?

Why can't I kiss you on the dance floor?

I wish that it could be like that

Why can't we be like that?

58

'Cause I'm yours."

We were swinging mid-air. The crowd was applauding as loud as they could and I was having the time of my life with Edward. Just us, doing what we love with the person we love. I wish it would have stayed like this forever. We finish the song and sing the last line together.

"Why can't we be like that? Wish we could be like that"

The swing had reached the ground and we got off it. The audience had never been so loud for anyone in the history of this competition. I had watched every season before this one and no crowd had ever applauded this much. This was the right moment. I could feel it. There would have never been a better moment to do what I wanted to do. I turned towards Edward, put my hand on his cheek and kissed him. This was the moment I had been waiting for since we met. The moment our lips touched, we melted into a sweet, passionate kiss. The screams from the crowd were just a background noise now. My heart felt like it could explode any minute. He held my cheek as we continued to kiss. We both wanted this for a long time, we just never had the courage to do it. Slowly, we pulled away from the kiss. Edward smiled at me and said: "You have no idea how much I've wanted this."

He couldn't even imagine how much I wanted this too. The perfect performance and the perfect kiss, it felt like I was living a fairy tale. I had found my prince and we would live happily ever after. Everything was perfect. It was only me, Edward and the immense love that we felt for each other. Nothing could have ruined this moment.

Until I heard it.

A gun shot.

Chapter ten

-----------------------------The end-------------------------------

It's been an hour since I left the hospital after the shooting. Pictures of it were still haunting my head. The screams that weren't happy screams anymore, they were screams of fear. The bullets flying in the air, getting anyone who wasn't lucky enough to dodge it. But mostly the blood. I could still see the image of the love of my life, lying in a pool of his own blood after getting shot in the stomach.

"Edward please stay with me. The paramedics are on their way. Please baby stay with me. I'm doing everything I can to stop the bleeding. Please don't leave me. I need you Edward, I need you to hold on, please. Think about how many picnics we could go on after you recover. Think about the adventures we'll live together if you just hold on for me. Please Edward. You'll be alright soon. The doctors will stop the bleeding and you'll be okay. Keep your eyes open baby."

I was sobbing while trying to stop the bleeding. He was dying. He was dying right in front of me and there's nothing I could do to help him. His eyes were slowly closing.

"Baby please, keep your eyes open for me, please. I need you Edward keep your fucking eyes open for god's sake. Focus on me baby, you'll be okay soon. No no no don't close them, no baby please."

I took his hand in mine and cried over his body that was fighting so hard to stay with me.

"I love you Edward, I love you more than anything. Please stay with me."

He was not strong enough to say it back, but with the last strength that he had, he squeezed my hand two times. His fingers let go off my hand and I couldn't feel his pulse anymore. The love of my life had just died in front of my eyes.

I was walking back home, my head filled with images of him, his lifeless body laying in my arms as I cried. I cried so much that I didn't think I still had any tears. He was gone. He was gone forever. We never got to experience all the things I had planned to do. We would have won for sure. With the money, we could have gone on a vacation to Paris, the most romantic city in the world. But no. A bastard had to shoot him and kill him. A depressed bastard that wanted to die, but had to take people with him. He had to take the love of my life with him. I wouldn't have given one fuck if that son of a bitch had died alone. But he took 20 people with him. One of those people was Edward. His funeral was going to be tomorrow morning. The only thing that I had, that belonged to him, was the suit I was wearing. It was covered in blood, his blood. When I got home, my mom was sitting on the couch waiting for me. When she saw me, she ran towards me crying, thanking god that I was okay. All of my sisters were fine too. My eyes were numb, I couldn't cry and the shock would probably never leave me. There was nothing I could do to get the feeling of numbness and destruction out of my mind, so I just went to bed.

This morning was the day of Edward's funeral. Last night, I dreamt of him. We were in the park where we ate together. He was sitting on a swing, just like we were during our performance. Then he got up. He was wearing the blue suit but it was covered in blood. The wound was open. It's like he was dying in front of me again. But this time, I could help him. I healed his wound in my dream. All I wanted was to be able to go back in time and really heal it. I would do anything just to be with him again. To hear his laugh one more time. To see him little dimples when he smiled. To see those green eyes, those beautiful green eyes of his one more time. I would give everything I have. After the shooting, the news reported all of the deaths. My phone was blowing up from notifications of people on twitter, saying that they knew how sad I was and that it was going to get better. But they knew nothing. This feeling is never going to go away. Every time I close my eyes, I see his lifeless body in my arm. I see the paramedics taking him from me and telling me that there was nothing I could have done to save him. But that's not true. I should have died last night. The bullet was directed towards me. Edward saw it soon enough to jump in front of me and save me. It was all my fault. I wish it would've been me instead, I really do. He didn't deserve to die. His soul was too pure and kind to die of such a horrible death. And today I had to sit with people that knew him, watch him get put six feet under the ground and go home. I had to keep living. My heart was still beating, but his wasn't. His heart hadn't beaten for the last twelve hours and it's never going to beat again. His eyes will never open again. No one will ever hear his beautiful voice again. It was late and I had to get ready for the funeral. I put on a black suit and brushed my teeth. The strength I had was not enough to do anything with my hair or even take a shower. The door opened and my mom walked into my room. "How are you sweetheart?"

That is the stupidest question you could ask someone after they lost the love of their life. How do you think I'm doing? Do you really think I'm doing fine after seeing Edward die in my arms? I ignored her question and went downstairs. I didn't want them to come to the funeral, my mom knew it. I didn't need anyone there to comfort me, because nothing could ever comfort me. I got in my car and went to the church. When I walked in, Edward's mom, Anne, was crying in front of her son's closed coffin. I didn't have the courage to walk up to her. If she only knew that her son died to save me, she would hate me. She probably already hates me since I got my chance to say goodbye to him and she didn't. I stayed in the back of the church the whole time. After it ended, I went to the cemetery. One of his friends said something for Edward. Then it was his mother's turn: "I've never seen him happier than in these last weeks since he started this competition. He told me about this boy that he had met. He never mentioned his name, he just mentioned that he had beautiful blue eyes and that he was in love with him. Edward always had a hard time with being happy. When we adopted him, we knew that he wasn't happy. We've loved him more than anything in this world. He was our sun. I know that boy that made him happy is here. So, if you're here, I want to thank you. I want to thank you for making my boy so happy, for bringing his gorgeous smile back, thank you." She started crying again, kissed Edward's coffing and sat back. I walked up to the front and sat next to her. When she saw me, she pulled into me into a hug and started to sob on my shoulder: "Thank you, thank you so much for keeping him happy." I hugged her tightly while she cried her loss on me.

"I know it's a big request, but could I have some time alone with Edward?"

"Sure darling." She got up and gestured everyone to follow her towards the other side of the cemetery. I walked up to Edward's coffin. It was a black shiny coffin.

"Hey baby. I miss you a lot. Yesterday was the best and the worst night of my life. I didn't get the chance to thank you for the swing, it was an amazing surprise. So, thank you for that and thank you for saving my life. All the people here today probably knew you for way longer than I did, but I'm sure there's no one here that loved you like I did. Our first kiss on the stage, in front of all those people, was my way of showing you how much I love you. It's going to be really hard for me, now that you're gone. One thing that I never told you, was that I never had my first kiss. I had never kissed someone before you and I'm so glad I waited. I love you so

much Edward. I know you can't say it back, but if you're some-
how, somewhere, listening to me right now, I know that you want
to say it back. I promise you, everyday from now on, I will live
for the both of you. I will visit all the places I wanted to visit with
you, I will write you songs and sing them to you, even if you can't
hear me. And when the day comes, when we meet again, we can
make some new memories together. I miss you so much Edward
and I know you would want me to stay strong, I'm really trying,
but it's just so hard. You were my everything. These past weeks
where I got to know you, were the best ones of my life. You will
forever be the best part of my life. You shouldn't have jumped in
front of me yesterday. That bullet should have hit me. I'm so sorry
that I couldn't do anything to help you, I really am. I'm going to
visit you every single day. There won't be one day where you'll
have to be alone here. I will bring you daisies, just like I did on
our first date. We will meet again and I will love you forever Edward. You were the peak of my existence.

© 2021, Sofia Rizzo
Printed and published by:
BoD - Books on Demand, Norderstedt
ISBN: 9783754301210